Praise for
JOSHUA DALTON

"In Joshua Dalton's winning collection of stories and tweets about feeling like a loser, technology is a weapon of self-destruction, love is the highest form of self-hatred, and mental health is an oxymoron. *I Hate You, Please Read Me* offers an honest and aching voice, steeped in absurdity. It drew from me loud, painful laughter that scared my dog."

**Jennifer Wortman, author of *This. This.
This. Is. Love. Love. Love.***

"It was raining and I was carrying my cat around in a blanket while looking for an Olive Garden—this was the dream I'd had after being up till 4 a.m. reading Joshua Dalton's book. Coincidence?"

Brian Alan Ellis, author of *Bad Poet*

"Joshua nails this sensation of being so 'wrong' in the eyes of 'society,' but he harnesses that wrongness as a form of power. Funny, assaulting, and fluid, *I Hate You, Please Read Me* is a great book."

Joe Halstead, author of *West Virginia*

"Joshua Dalton elevates cyber spiraling to an art form."

Brooks Sterritt, author of
The History of America in My Lifetime

"[*I Hate You, Please Read Me*] is for anyone who has a reasonless life, but finds enjoyment in their reasonless life."

Noah Cicero, author of *Las Vegas*
Bootlegger: Empire of Self-Importance

"[Joshua] Dalton is transforming feelings of inadequacy and exclusion into a palatable product for general consumption. His irreverent treatment of serious mental issues introduces an element of the absurd, which translates into comedy, which both distracts from and complements the depressive tone of the book. [*I Hate You, Please Read Me* is] funny, and it's dark, and it's usually fucked up."

Entropy

"For those of us left wanting after the cancellation of *Crazy Ex-Girlfriend* after only four brilliant seasons, Joshua Dalton's book fills that void."

Charlene Elsby, author of *Affect*

"Joshua Dalton has such a brilliant voice—both despondent and hilarious, cruel and empathetic. These stories are filled with a kind of charming despair that rings so deeply, horribly true. This is a book that walks a fine line between pain and humor, and balances there perfectly. This is one that will stick with you."

Cathy Ulrich, author of *Ghosts of You*

I HATE YOU,
PLEASE READ ME

Also from
HOUSE OF VLAD PRESS

Hotel Alexander / Rebekah Morgan

Bad Poet / Brian Alan Ellis

Body High / Jon Lindsey

Horror Vacui / Shy Watson

*Please Buy This Book So I Can Feel Validated
& (Finally) Love Myself* / Homeless

All Must Go / Kevin Sterne

Noah Cicero's Wild Kingdom / Noah Cicero

Hot Young Stars / Sophie Jennis

*Your Glass Head Against the Brick
Parade of Now Whats* / Sam Pink

I Still Love You, Peggy Bundy / Justin Grimbol

Wallop / Nathaniel Kennon Perkins

Calm Face / Bud Smith

I

HATE

YOU,

PLEASE

READ

ME

A Book by

JOSHUA DALTON

HOUSE OF VLAD PRESS
Super Fun Land • USA

A HOUSE OF VLAD BOOK
© 2021 by Joshua Dalton

Printed in Super Fun Land, USA

First Edition: February, 2021

Book design: Percy Hearst
Author photograph: © Joshua Dalton

Joshua Dalton's Twitter: @postitbreakup

houseofvladpress.com / Twitter: @HouseofVlad

houseofvlad.bigcartel.com

ISBN: 9781534721357

for anyone who's had an FP

Contents

The Showrunner

But it's okay that I'm an unemployed screenwriter back living with my parents, because one day I'll turn this into a great sitcom.

Like the episode where Max Collins (my TV alter ego) convinces a guy he likes that his parents are living with *him* and not vice versa, but after several comical mishaps ("What's with all the baby pictures?") the truth emerges. Max, rejected, asks his mother something definitively childish, like "Can you tuck me in?" Canned laughter, credits roll.

And maybe one where Grant, Max's successful brother, visits and, realizing how depressed Max has become, waits until their parents are off-screen visiting relatives before stocking the house with a keg and lots of friends. (My brother—Max's brother, I mean—can always find friends.) Max, distraught after bombing yet another job interview, arrives home to the thudding bass of whatever's popular. He acts like he's enjoying this "killer party," but really he's having trouble just choking down sips of beer and is completely flustered by all the people, so when someone drunkenly shatters his mother's favorite duck figurine, Max sends everyone home.

Grant is all, "But bro, I did this for you. I was trying to give you back your college experience," and Max tearfully (but in a masculine manner) admits, "That's the thing, Grant. I never had the college experience. I studied my ass off all four years, turned down every invitation, and now I've failed anyway. Not only at being a screenwriter, but at having a life."

The audience will "awwww" at this special moment, and *Entertainment Weekly* will declare: "While the show at first seemed sophomoric, tonight's airing of 'Surprise Kegger' proved that creator Marshall Crawford, talented beyond his years, actually knows how to write characters with heart."

Unless the network gets bored watching it.

(I certainly get bored living it.)

Mr. Executive might say, "Marshall, while we at the network were thrilled about your unprecedented Emmy nod for 'Surprise Kegger,' is Max ever going to get a life? You can only make so many episodes about a guy watching TV with his parents."

Because I refuse to develop a bad reputation—I'm going to be given lucrative development deals and glowing write-ups in *Variety*—my reply to this challenge will be a calm, vibrant smile. I'll explain how, in an upcoming episode, Max reconnects with the two guys from his study group (known for our—*their*—epic library marathons). That will help provide the social life Max has desperately been missing. Although, the network might worry—like my therapist—that this is not enough.

Mr. Executive might say, "A study group? That's great for one episode, but not a whole show. Also, when is he going to get a boyfriend? What's the point of having a gay protagonist who never hooks up?" And if that feedback wouldn't feel bad enough, Mr. Executive might add, going in for the kill, "Maybe the show needs a new direction?"

I will start sweating, but thanks to the corrective procedure I can finally afford, I won't drench my shirt. As my new buddy Chuck Lorre will have warned me, the network's idea of a new direction is never good. I'll have to respond as quickly and cleverly as a character on TV.

"Exactly," I'll say. (As I've learned in "the business," it's always best to start a pitch by agreeing with the network.) "So that's why, in the next episode, Max decides to place an ad on Craigslist... or Twitter." (Any mention of social networking is guaranteed to pique the executive's interest.)

In the cable biopic they'll one day make about me, this is where I'll get my biggest close-up: the moment I turn my charming little show into a smash hit.

"Max will tweet, 'There are thousands of others out there like me, with college degrees but no prospects. We could band together, form our own community.'"

Mr. Executive looks intrigued, even puts down his iPad's stylus.

"We'll put out a casting call for these new characters," I continue. "Four new friends, one of them a gay guy. So I—*Max!*—can finally get laid. And they can all hang out in Max's basement, and when we need new material in later seasons, these friends can have their own 'obnoxious parent' storylines. In season six or seven, if the whole 'adult kids stuck at home' concept is played out, these friends can all move in together and then—"

Mr. Executive says, "You've got yourself a second season."

Of course, I'll doubt this retooling. In the limousine ride back to my new LA penthouse, I'll wonder about the Crawford—I mean Collins—family dynamic. Wasn't that the heart of the show?

But once we film this pivotal cast-changing episode, which I'll say in interviews was planned all along, and once I see the new gang assembled—the gay guy, the hot chick, the nerdy chick, the non-threatening black guy—I'll know that this was where the show was headed all along.

In this arena, I'll know best. I'll no longer be a sweaty loser who gets so nervous during job interviews that he can't even get hired by Starbucks; who stays up until 4 a.m. watching reruns of shitty sitcoms, knowing he'll never write something good enough for CBS, much less HBO; who feels utterly crushed by the massive student loan debt it took to get this worthless fucking screenwriting degree.

I'll be the showrunner.

I *am* the showrunner.

(Just as soon as I move out and write the pilot.)

My Problem Areas Are
My Body and My Mind

I miss thinking that the best part of life was ahead of me,
and not just something I saw on TV

# # #

how many carbs are in depression?

# # #

I can't tell the difference between
perseverance and obsession

# # #

MTV True Life: Sometimes When I Get Scared and Dra-
matically Flip on Every Light in My Apartment, I Hope I
Actually Find an Intruder, Because at Least a Home Inva-
sion Would Be a Break from This Crushing Monotony

# # #

though I desperately seek happiness,
I think I've always worried that it's "basic"

# # #

I'm 10% existential horror, 20% television, 30% please love me, and 40% OMG I hate myself

# # #

my achy breaky brain

# # #

I love when it's storming and the sky looks how I feel

# # #

the Wellness Cop pounds on my door as he screams, "ARE YOU LIVING YOUR BEST LIFE IN THERE?!"

# # #

8 billion people and I had to be this one

# # #

feeling squirmy like my insides want out

# # #

it's overwhelming needing to improve myself in *so* many ways just to be a C-minus human being

# # #

does life also feel this bad for other people, but they're better than I am at coping? or, for other people, does life not feel this bad?

# # #

"no pressure!"—pressure

# # #

does this obsession make me look fat?

# # #

I'm in hell, which I don't even believe in

# # #

"having a really hard time today"—me, every single day

# # #

almost choked on a French fry and thought,
good, I deserve this, and kept eating French fries

# # #

more mess from me—just what y'all ordered

# # #

I think, therefore I'm sad

# # #

THE SUN:
it's time to wake up

ME:
can you explode already?

# # #

the Tower of Terror ride at Disney, except it's you
with your coworkers in an ordinary elevator

# # #

I'll quit thinking negative thoughts when I'm brain-dead

# # #

yeah I live in the moment, just not until it's passed

# # #

if only I could make my emotions fuck off the way
award show bands can play people off stage

# # #

I can't tell the difference between
a breakdown and a breakthrough

# # #

biting my nails to punish my hands for the actions I take

# # #

why look for work when feeling sorry
for myself is a full-time job?

# # #

SPOILER ALERT: nothing matters

# # #

sings ["We Can't Stop"]
and we can sob
and we will sob
can't you see it's we who cry all night?
can't you see it's we who rue our life?

# # #

ready to be pessimistic about something new

# # #

there's no place like home when no place feels like home

# # #

keep getting hit with a hopeless feeling, so heavy it could crush me, and I rush to tell myself, "things aren't that bad, you're OK, just keep going," a mantra I repeat until the hopeless feeling passes... but it always comes back

# # #

sometimes I fantasize about eating until I'm too fat to lift for the rescue crane that will never come

# # #

most of the conversations I have happen only in my mind

# # #

I feel great*

*great pressure to feel better

# # #

Honey, I Shrunk My Self-Esteem!

# # #

wish my pain was less cliché

# # #

being conflicted about everything is going great / terrible

# # #

SOME PEOPLE:
the glass is half-empty

OTHER PEOPLE:
the glass is half-full

ME:
I broke the glass

# # #

terrified that I've already lived up to my full potential

# # #

felt too much then ate too much

# # #

CHANDLER (from *Friends*):
could life *be* any less meaningful?

# # #

whenever I finish writing something, I feel like I don't know where it came from, and that it's never going to happen again—like it was written by a different person entirely, who only inhabits my body a few times a year

# # #

stare into the abyss and the abyss says, "this is a mirror"

# # #

I'm a hemorrhoid on the asshole of the universe

# # #

HOW ARE YOU TODAY?

"good" = "meh"
"okay" = "bad"
"not great" = "extremely shitty"
"bad" = "call for help"

# # #

wish I could douche my skull to clean my brain

# # #

extremely "working hard, or hardly working?" dad joke voice sad to be awake, or awake to be sad?

# # #

I feel like a shitty first draft

# # #

it's not that nobody cares, it's just that nobody can help

# # #

crying on the outside, screaming on the inside

# # #

LIFE: a Choose-Your-Own-Bullshit Adventure

# # #

protect me from what I want, from what I don't want, and
from wanting or not wanting things in general

# # #

when will someone cure feelings?

# # #

yeah I've made mistakes, but they weren't canon

# # #

gonna start saying I'm "between" things instead of not
having them, like "I'm between boyfriends right now" and
"I'm between writing jobs right now" and "I'm between
good moods right now"

# # #

instead of "good morning," we should say
"sorry for your loss"

# # #

finally figured out what my sign is—it's STOP

# # #

sometimes my apartment feels like
a trap from the *Saw* movies

# # #

love reading recipes for food I'll never make as part of
diets I'll never follow for the life I'll never have

# # #

be myself? more like flee myself

# # #

keep waiting to feel good enough to do something,
but apparently the only way to feel better
is to do something

# # #

taking a break from hating myself to masturbate

# # #

what the fuck do you expect me to do
with all of these emotions?

# # #

might go to bed early, might jump off the balcony

# # #

late for my next disappointment

you can call it a pity party, but it feels like a funeral

ME:
I'm sick

COWORKER:
aw, get well soon

ME:
no, I mean I think I'm mentally ill

COWORKER:
oh. get well soon?

ME:
actually, I've felt like this my whole life, and nothing hel—

COWORKER:
new phone, who dis?

I wish I was as excited about anything as the guy in the
catheter commercial is excited about catheters

somehow always hungry, despite being full of rage

###

I've got a bad feeling about bliss

# # #

still in shock every year that
I don't get off for summer break

# # #

got cast in the role of human, but I'm a bad actor

# # #

since it's after midnight, it's a new day, so I'm still gonna
say I made it all of yesterday without crying

# # #

behind and before me, an ocean of days
with no coastline in sight

# # #

I wanna punch something as hard as I can,
but without leaving my couch

# # #

not a day goes by where I don't think back to the creative,
hopeful, confident little kid I was and wonder how the hell
I ended up a boring miserable loser with no one to love

# # #

if worrying burned calories, I'd be so fucking fit

# # #

starting to suspect that watching
Real Housewives isn't good for me

# # #

my brain is like an abandoned town in a horror movie,
where happiness's car broke down

# # #

kid-me would hate adult-me so much

# # #

constantly nostalgic for things that I didn't enjoy

# # #

saw a commercial about removing hard water stains
and thought, *maybe the water in my body is hard,
and that's why I'm so difficult?"*

# # #

all week I wait for the weekend as if then I'll be happy

# # #

weather report: cloudy with a chance of meaninglessness

# # #

I feel too exhausted from doing nothing all day
to do something now

# # #

binge-watch me binge-eat everything in my apartment

# # #

the movie of my life would just be
montages of me crying on my couch

# # #

ME:
I can't find meaningful work, I'm running out of money,
and I can't even remember the last time I had sex

DOCTOR:
sounds like a chemical imbalance

# # #

ready for this week to be over and also my life

# # #

so sick of being me all by myself

# # #

nothing makes me sadder than pressure to be happy

# # #

if I use Postmates anymore this week,
someone is gonna call the cops

# # #

9 out of 10 intrusive thoughts agree…

# # #

thinking about other people whose dinner is also the high-
light of their day, and feeling sad for us all...
but at least I have tacos!

# # #

need to be thinner, more symmetrical and less human

# # #

keep waking up on the wrong side of the ground

# # #

sure, I'm shitty, but life is shitty too...
there's shittiness on both sides

# # #

my brain is a bingo machine with no winning numbers

# # #

pleased to accept the Oscar for Best Director
of a shit-show called *My Life*

# # #

I feel obligated to consider my isolated and unfulfilling life
as basically okay, because at least I'm not homeless, or a
refugee in war-torn wherever

# # #

trying to drink enough water to drown out my thoughts

# # #

ANYTHING:
happens

ME:
I've let down everyone
and ruined everything

# # #

to cry is human; to ugly cry is divine

# # #

I had a decent day, so catastrophe must be imminent

# # #

"but this time it's different!"—it's never different

# # #

part of me thinks having to minimize how
excruciating my existence feels is unfair;
part of me thinks I'm just a spoiled brat

# # #

just need to lose 40 pounds and finish a book
and find a boyfriend by 5 o'clock today

# # #

it only hurts when I'm awake to feel it

###

counting on the existence of a powerful future-me,
someone who won't drink or smoke weed or eat fried
food, someone who writes and exercises and meditates,
someone not actually me

###

ME, to the mirror: who the fuck do you think you are?

###

will my "authentic self" please stand up?

###

there are a lot of photos where I was smiling,
but only a couple where I was happy

###

too tired of not-being-enough to not-be-enough today

###

I'm afraid that I'll never catch up, or do anything lasting,
or be anyone great

###

my happiness is in the Black Lodge with the Good Dale

###

hit my goal weight by breaking my scale

# # #

when has something being a bad idea ever stopped me?

# # #

can't decide whether I feel more like garbage or shit

# # #

my brain is a busted, squeaky shopping cart
I'm pushing through a grocery store in hell

# # #

I would give anything to go back to that "kid watching
MTV and thinking they'll grow up to be free and wild and
actually happy like all the spring breakers" age

# # #

what do you mean that blowing dozens of dollars on
drinks in an attempt to "go out and have fun like a 'normal
person'" can't fill the gaping void within?

# # #

good news when I'm in a bad mood feels much worse
than bad news when I'm in a good mood

# # #

my superpower: making people close to me
feel uncomfortable

Batman the Millennial

Batman scrolling through Instagram on his Batphone, scowling at Superman's selfies. He accidentally likes and then quickly un-likes a Valencia-filtered picture of Superman and Lois sharing avocado toast.

Batman perched on a skyscraper, listening to a meditation app. "Imagine your thoughts as fish in a stream. Notice them as they swim by, but don't catch them." A bank alarm sounds. Sighing, Batman leaps.

Batman ordering Postmates while Alfred's on vacation. Then he remembers the whole secret identity thing. He cancels his Chipotle burrito and logs out as Batman, then logs in as Bruce Wayne and makes the same order. Probably no one will notice, right?

Batman squeezing into his Batsuit, worried that he has gained weight.

Batman noticing a parking ticket on the Batmobile's windshield. He considers asking Commissioner Gordon to make it go away. But wouldn't that be as bad as picking up a gun? Still, you never saw real cops getting tickets. Would he ever be appreciated?

Batman swiping left on Vicki Vale and right on Selina Kyle. No match. Disappointed, he closes Tinder and opens Words with SuperFriends.

Batman on a treadmill, watching CNN on mute. President Luthor is giving a press conference about the coming nuclear war. Batman wonders if he should get involved, perhaps become more politically active. He turns on *Real Housewives* instead.

Batman reaching under the Batcomputer to unplug the Batrouter. He counts to fifteen and then plugs it back in. If this doesn't fix it, he'll have to call Comcast.

Batman eating probiotic yogurt, wondering if it actually works or if it's just a marketing scam. His phone chimes with a Facebook invite to the Justice League Christmas party. He clicks *Maybe*, but he knows he won't attend.

Batman Venmoing Robin $200. He adds a memo: *This is the last time.*

Batman taking Advil, then wondering if he takes it too often. He googles *how often you can take Advil?* and scrolls through the WebMD page for liver failure, briefly feeling worried. Then he opens an incognito tab and navigates PornHub, fingers reaching into his Batbriefs.

Batman pausing mid-punch to ask Bane about his workout. "You do interval training, right?"

Batman chuckling at the Joker's latest tweet, before stopping himself and looking around to make sure no one saw him. (Of course no one saw; he's in the Batsubmarine.)

Batman re-re-watching *The Office* on Netflix, wondering if he should get a job at WayneCorp. "Maybe I could make work friends."

Batman waking up sweaty and worried, like the walls are closing in. He tries taking a deep breath, then panics that he can't breathe. Frantic, he digs through his nightstand and finds a bottle of Xanax. He takes one, then another. For a moment he feels calm, almost okay. Then his phone chimes that it's time to wake up, so he throws it at a wall, shattering it into Batpieces.

Regression

My therapist looked sickly the last time I saw him—all pale and clammy. I wanted to leave, but I knew I wouldn't get my money back.

Instead of taking the chair across from him like usual, I sat on the couch by a wilting potted plant and a bookshelf full of textbooks and Freud figurines. "Gifts from patients," Dr. Chives had explained to me. The weird thing was how many he had, like every patient who'd given their therapist that Freud action figure thought they were the first person to have the idea.

The couch squeaked as I tried getting comfortable. I'd walked in agitated and it was only getting worse now, having to deal with a lumpy couch and a leaking therapist—water pooled in the twin reservoirs of his puffy lower eyelids as snot dripped slowly from his nose. He wasn't talking, so I cleared my throat loudly to prompt him.

"Good afternoon," he said finally, like he was just now emerging from a coma. His voice creaked, so dry compared to his wet face. The room had at least five tissue boxes, and I desperately wished he would grab one.

"You OK?" I asked, trying to sound concerned.

"Well..." Dr. Chives said, "actually..."

"Because I'm not," I said.

Dr. Chives sighed, his nose whistling. "Do you want to talk about it?"

I launched into my usual monologue: "I thought I did everything right, you know. I studied hard, always got good grades. I was bad at sports, but I did student council. I got into a decent college, graduated with only a small loan. And I'm working now, finally got my own place—"

Dr. Chives nodded, like he'd heard all this before. Which, in fairness, I guess he had. But couldn't he at least pretend to look interested, instead of just nauseous?

"Anyway," I said, "everything feels extra pointless right now. I'm not saying I'm suicidal, but I'm not *not* saying it either."

I looked at Dr. Chives, waiting for him to jump on the whole suicide thing. Picking up on my glare, he finally said, "Have you shared these feelings with anyone else? Family, friends?"

"My family is worthless," I said. "My parents are busy with work, my brother's never around—they're totally consumed with themselves."

Dr. Chives stifled a sneeze.

"As far as friends, I talk to coworkers... sometimes...

and I've attempted the dating apps. But I can't say that I'm really close to anyone."

"Why do you think you have trouble making friends?"

"I don't know. Ask them."

"Hmm..." Dr. Chives finally blew his nose, which stained the tissue red.

Yuck, I thought. But I pressed on: "Also, it's like, what do you even say? What can you even talk about?"

"You find it hard to talk to people?"

"It's not that. I mean, yes, but, that's not what I'm trying to say... It all feels like small talk to me, no matter what the topic is. Like, what difference does it make how many siblings they have or what their job is? And even the things I like, there's nothing to say about them. Like, 'Did you see that show on Netflix, wasn't it great?' 'Yes, it sure was.' We're all just—" I made the jerk-off motion.

Dr. Chives didn't respond, didn't even crack a smile.

I continued: "A lot of the time, I feel like everything's on pause. Like everything's temporary, not really *real*. Like I'm on vacation from my actual life, but a horrible one, in the world's worst hotel... Are you listening?"

He coughed into a tissue—the same bloody one—not even bothering to get another. "Yes," he said, "sorry. As you might have noticed, I haven't been feeling well."

"You shouldn't come to work sick," I said. "You could be contagious."

"You're right. Actually, I meant to bring this up last time, but—"

"Are we really going to talk about you now?" I asked. "I mean, I'm sorry you're sick, but it is my appointment and all, and this isn't exactly cheap."

Dr. Chives nodded, closing his eyes.

And that was the last time I saw my therapist.

The Apple Doesn't Fall
Far from the Trauma

Michael, eight years old, knew he was going to die.

Attending his grandma's funeral had been traumatic enough: the weeping relatives, her pale corpse. But then, only three days later, Dad accidentally backed his truck over Michael's dog.

Michael's parents tried comforting him as he cradled Chester's limp, bloody body. They buried Chester in a flower bed.

"It's the circle of life," Dad said. "Like when we go hunting."

"Like *The Lion King*," Mom added.

Michael said, "That doesn't really help."

His parents told him not to think about it, but mortality latched onto Michael's brain like a tick, sucking the liveliness from his mind.

He didn't tell any of his classmates about his growing despair. He didn't start cutting himself or wearing all black—not that Mom would have let him anyway—but he did start writing little "cries for help."

At the bottom of a worksheet about the water cycle, he wrote "WLATWEWBHMLA?" ("Why learn about this when earth won't be here much longer anyway?") And on the back of a Mother's Day card: "SYMMAYOTLM, DTMYLF?" ("Since you're my Mom and you're obligated to love me, doesn't that make your love fake?")

Michael wrote only in acronyms; he knew that if anyone realized what was in his brain, he would get locked up in a hospital.

Eventually, Michael stopped caring. He gave up on the acronyms and tried to write about himself, but like everything else in his life, the writing soon felt pointless, so he shot himself in the face with his Dad's rifle, painting his bedroom walls red.

Michael, slumped over like a headless drunk, looked and felt dead.

For months, his parents kept the bedroom sealed like a shrine. They filled the house with air fresheners and binge-watched TV. Eventually, their therapist—and a recovering housing market—encouraged Michael's parents to move. That meant finally cleaning his old room.

When they opened the door, pinching their nostrils to block out the stench, they found an exceptionally ugly baby. The baby was lying in a pool of coagulated blood. It had grown from Michael's corpse.

Mom and Dad assumed they had snapped, that this house had made them crazy. That the baby wasn't real.

Just to make sure, they put the baby in an Ikea bag and carried it to a nearby gas station. They asked the cashier if he could see the baby. The cashier nodded and suggested they get a carwash. Mom said, "No, no thank you," and cried tears of joy.

They named the baby Mikey, then moved cross-country to a small town. They never questioned Mikey's origins; they saw him as a miracle, a second chance, an opportunity to raise their child right.

Mikey, hardly crying and never getting sick, grew to be a toddler. He seemed healthy and happy. After tucking him in at night, Mom and Dad hugged each other in the doorway of his room, congratulating themselves on parenting so well.

One morning, Mikey used alphabet blocks to spell out "IHMAIWTD" ("I hate myself and I want to die.")

Though Michael had killed himself at eight years old, Mikey made it only to four.

He used a jump rope to hang himself from the swing set in their backyard. There wasn't any blood. It was just Mikey, twirling in the wind like a zombie tether ball.

The parents, realizing they had somehow ruined another child, locked themselves in their bedroom.

Then they burned the house down.

In the backyard, beneath the swing set's ashes, Mikey's limbs stretched tendril-like into roots.

From his stomach, a tree erupted.

And there were all these tiny babies.

They hung from the tree's limbs like crying apples.

All of them screaming.

The Internet Is Killing Me,
But Way Too Slowly

YOU:
I'm starting a podcast about my Instagram,
which is screenshots of the memes
I cross-post on Facebook and Twitter

ME:
I'm suicidal

# # #

every post is a cry for the help I need to log off

# # #

depression is my peanut butter,
and compulsive tweeting is my jam

# # #

I wish there was a social network where people only
posted about their fears and disappointments, a place
where everyone was feeling much worse than me
instead of much better

# # #

glad you made a Facebook event
just to let me know I wasn't invited

# # #

Siri, add "I hate when someone with a ton of followers
who's never going to follow me back has such good
tweets that I have to follow them anyway" to the list:
Thoughts That Make Me Hate Who I've Become

# # #

ironic that being the first person to actually die from lack
of attention would be a great way to get attention

# # #

people will like your tweets about being crazy,
but will not like your actual craziness

# # #

stare into the abyss and the abyss asks you
to "like and subscribe"

# # #

when I unfollow someone, then follow them, then unfollow
them again—that's the real me

# # #

maybe if I find someone to cancel, I'll feel better

# # #

can't I just, like, order some stability from Amazon?

#

I'm just a boy, refreshing my Twitter notifications,
asking for strangers to love me

#

keep opening new tabs, unsure what I'm searching for…
possibly a "meaning"?

#

sure it was a corporate AI marketing ploy, but Spotify
Wrapped was also the most interest someone has ever
shown in my taste of music

#

ME:
I wish people would respond to every single tweet

ALSO ME:
sends too many tweets in a row for anyone to keep up

#

when I tweet a long thread baring my soul and it doesn't
get attention, I start shame-spiraling, convinced that
everyone hates me now, and end up deleting the thread
and returning to tweeting in a style that has gotten likes
before—that's the real me

#

congratulates self publicly and calls it accountability

###

whoever's depression tweets get
the most likes wins the prize*

*the prize is more depression

###

soon as the pain that Twitter causes me outweighs the
temporary high that getting likes gives me, it's over for
"it's over for you bitches" tweets

###

feel completely disconnected despite
constantly being online

###

when I was born, I couldn't care for myself,
and I had no way to get attention other than crying…
30 years later, I'm exactly the same

###

my self-retweets are not endorsements

###

who's coming to my Zoom funeral?

###

can't stay off my phone long enough to charge it

###

my thoughts are my children, and my tweets are my
children's dance recitals, so when you give my tweets
"profile clicks" instead of likes, it's as if you're asking,
"whose kids are THOSE?!" without clapping

# # #

[something self-deprecating and mildly amusing
to mask the intense horror]

# # #

sings ["How's It Gonna Be?"]
gonna give myself retweets again
the self-love of oblivion

# # #

ignoring a Facebook friend request from death

# # #

feeling annoyed at people who tweet sincerely about
things that don't involve them while I tweet
ironically about nothing but myself

# # #

the best part of being in the mental hospital
was not having internet

# # #

0 likes, 0 retweets, 0 hope

# # #

jeez, it's almost as if constant affirmation
is too much to expect

# # #

I searched myself today, to see if I still feel

# # #

can't wait to not read your book!

# # #

attention is my blood, and I am hemorrhaging

# # #

the lie that people who killed themselves are "resting,"
"in a better place," or "finally at peace," promotes more
suicide attempts… but RIP celebrity I never met!

# # #

blocking anybody who posts good news
without a trigger warning

# # #

feeling "ordered a product from a Facebook ad" bad

# # #

when I delete my post, I'm a little kid again, sure that you
can't see me if I cover my own eyes

# # #

do podcasts count as friends?

# # #

"the people who leave a thumbs up care a little... but the
people who leave a heart are the ones who *really* care"—
me, a completely normal person, thinking about
responses to my Facebook post

# # #

it's called an Instagram "story" because it's fictional

# # #

found out someone died and thought,
I'm glad they followed me back first

# # #

live, laugh, love through your Sims character
while your real life decays

# # #

I've clicked the refresh button for whole months of my life

# # #

any time I'm in danger of feeling okay
I can just log on to social media
to remember that I'm not okay
and never will be

# # #

the opposite of following isn't blocking, it's indifference

# # #

when I shame-spiral and delete my tweets in an effort to
punish / destroy myself, only to post the same tweets
again once I'm feeling "better" because I still think they're
funny and I still want attention, only to re-delete them the
next time my self-hatred becomes uncontrollable—
that's the real me

# # #

MTV True Life: My Contacts List is Mostly Relatives

# # #

I really don't appreciate the implication that some of you
have better things to do than spend Saturday night alone
staring at your phone

# # #

there's infinite content and zero contentment

# # #

"no one has engaged with your tweet yet. please check
back later!" *checks back later* "no one has engaged with
your tweet yet... loser"

# # #

like my phone, I am usually drained,
and often on the verge of dying completely

# # #

I had to delete that pic of my face
because it was a pic of my face

# # #

bringing printed-out emails / texts / DMs to my therapist
like they're exhibits in court

# # #

I want the entire world to care
about what I have to say,
but I would never care about
what the entire world has to say

# # #

feel like your tweet about setting boundaries is a subtweet
against me, but maybe that's my own bad boundaries?

# # #

when I'm really hungry, even bad food tastes good...
and attention works the same way

# # #

I hate you, retweet me

# # #

busy liking the same post on four different platforms

# # #

what button do I push to make us friends?

# # #

I'm agoraphobic, but I still want an audience

# # #

probably it's more accurate to say
I live online than anywhere else

# # #

I tweet too much because I am too much

# # #

1 like = 1 more thing that won't fill the void within

# # #

Everything You Never Wanted to Know About Me and
Were Too Uninterested to Ask

# # #

I feel like my apartment's just a coffin with Wi-Fi

# # #

more concerned with being heard
than with having something to say

# # #

"I don't wanna see that!"—y'all re: my emotions /
me re: your successes

\# \# \#

kind of want to start a blog, kind of want to stand
in the middle of the highway

\# \# \#

I'm so vain, I probably think your tweet is about me

\# \# \#

new LinkedIn profile: help me pay for my funeral

\# \# \#

I need more attention-spackle for this hole I'll never patch

\# \# \#

stop attacking me with your joy

\# \# \#

if a tweet I'm proud of doesn't get a like,
I'll just like it myself (before deleting it)

\# \# \#

I keep forgetting that online relationships
are with irl people

\# \# \#

everyone's brand is the same: "tell me I'm worthy"

\# \# \#

sometimes I force myself not to like someone's tweet
because I've already liked so many of their tweets before,
and I don't want them to think I sit around waiting for their
tweets when actually I'm sitting around waiting for death
while leaving Twitter on in the background

# # #

took a selfie and the whole world
went blind prophylactically

# # #

and if he asks what I'm doing while I'm wasting time on
Reddit, I'll say "I'm reading," knowing he'll assume
I mean a book

# # #

I want to say it all RIGHT NOW and SO LOUD

# # #

when someone hasn't liked one of my tweets in a while
I try to think of something to "win them back"

# # #

can people who are happy just not?

# # #

restarting my Twitter account like this time it'll be alright,
like this time every tweet will be a gem

# # #

fell into a zit-popping video hole on YouTube

# # #

y'all are killing me with this lack of attention

# # #

sometimes I feel like my online presence is an actual
celebrity version of myself whose reputation
I have to carefully maintain

# # #

every tweet is a nude from the monster inside me

# # #

I saw an article about how technology damaged our
attention spans, but I couldn't finish it

# # #

how many likes would it take to make me like myself?

# # #

what I'd really like back is AOL Instant Messenger
(also, the last fifteen years)

# # #

social media is my social life / death

# # #

I check my phone like some people check locks

\# \# \#

wish I could be one of those people who only tweet
when they have something to say

\# \# \#

"it was a hot, hellish summer, the summer everyone had
a podcast, and I didn't know what I was doing online…"

\# \# \#

googling "healthy meals for one"
and "painless suicide methods"

\# \# \#

now streaming: my tears

\# \# \#

tfw you post something like "I'm so disgusting" or "the
world would be better off if I died" because you
desperately want someone to disagree with you
but instead you get a like

\# \# \#

sometimes I feel sorry for the people
who haven't blocked / muted me

\# \# \#

I can't tell the difference between thoughts I have
naturally that I then decide to tweet, and thoughts that I
think of only so I can tweet them

###

follow people more successful than you are so there's
always a new reason to feel inadequate

###

*I Think I Like This Tweet, But I Won't Know for Sure
Unless You Like It, Too: A Sickness*

###

YOU: emp-owered

ME: emp-ty

###

when I compulsively reply to famous tweeters I've
followed for years with the delusion that we're friends irl—
that's the real me.

###

I'll never achieve my dreams, but at least I can read
interviews with people who achieve theirs

###

have a feeling I can't hold in anymore →
tweet about it →
feel stupid for tweeting →
delete tweet and try to hold in feelings ↻

###

checking my phone as if it might have notifications
that didn't reach my computer

# # #

person with 10 followers:
I want more followers

person with 100 followers:
I want more followers

person with 1000 followers:
I want more followers

person with 10000 followers:
I want more followers

# # #

when I soft-block someone because I have a negative
feeling toward them and don't want to have them as a
follower anymore, but then get upset that they're no
longer following me—that's the real me

# # #

it's called a twitter "feed" because
we're starving for attention

# # #

googling "internet addiction" again

# # #

shedding followers like dandruff

\# \# \#

ME:
unfollows everyone even vaguely upsetting

ALSO ME:
"why is my timeline so boring?!"

\# \# \#

keep using up my allotment of validation
too early in the day

\# \# \#

I alternate between hating everyone
and worrying that everyone hates me

\# \# \#

I can't tell the difference between
oversharing and honesty

\# \# \#

YOU:
posts thirst traps

ME:
posts barf bait

\# \# \#

checking twitter while I drive because I want to quit my
phone but need a drastic intervention

\# \# \#

pitching a reboot of *Friends* called *Six People Sitting
Separately All Staring At Their Phones*

\# \# \#

I really, really, really, really, really, really, really need
to stay the fuck off Facebook

\# \# \#

followers come and followers go, but the futile pursuit of
external validation lasts forever

\# \# \#

what twitter, sex, and drinking have in common: anyone
who does it less than you is a loser, and anyone who
does it more than you is an addict

\# \# \#

expressing my feelings honestly instead of editing them
for maximum likes? in this economy?

\# \# \#

god I wish deleting myself was as easy
as deleting my tweets

Feeling Canceled Despite Never Actually Airing

"How's your day going?" the dentist asks.

"Shitty," I say, not looking up from Twitter on my phone.

"I hear that," the dentist says, shoving fingers in my mouth. "Some days are like"—he pauses for emphasis—"pulling teeth!"

He laughs, and I consider biting him.

The dentist finally finishes. "No cavities," he says, snapping off his gloves, "but... did you always have only one molar?"

"No," I tell him, wiping my mouth. "I mean, I don't think so."

He wheels towards me on his little rolling stool. "Also, it's not really my department, but... your ear lobes, were they always missing too?"

"Fuck." My ear lobes' absence hadn't been a hallucination. "Those crazy assholes on the internet were right."

He asks what I'm talking about.

"I'm disappearing," I explain. "I was cancelled for tweeting the word 'retarded,' and now I'm vanishing, bit by bit. The internet has cursed me."

The dentist frowns. "You really shouldn't say that word."

My traditional post-dentist milkshake tastes ashy and bitter, but I keep sucking on it anyway.

That's the kind of thing I would have turned into a tweet before.

For example: *My milkshake brings all the boys to the yard, and they're like, "this milkshake is disgusting."*

Or: *Maybe this sugar will fill the hole you left in my life.*

Lots of faintly witty, massively whiny ranting directed mostly at my wildly successful ex-boyfriend, who has me blocked and wouldn't see the tweets anyway.

Then one night, drunk and leaving voicemails in my ex's inbox—alternately begging for another chance and wishing he would get AIDS and die—I ended up (as I always do) back on Twitter.

I tweeted: *when it comes to love, I'm not just ignorant, I'm full-blown retarded.*

I had 63 followers then, most of them dead accounts. It was rare for me to get more than one like; if a tweet got two, I was ecstatic. So I wasn't used to getting notifications, wasn't prepared for how quickly shit can blow up.

I guess some advocacy group had created a Twitter bot that would retweet any uses of the word "retarded," and then this account's followers would descend to punish the offender with stories of differently-abled relatives and comparisons to the N-word. Some of these tweets were so lacking in self-awareness that they surely had to represent some super-awareness, something past irony. Like the woman who tweeted at me, a gay man: *don't say retarded, you fat fucking faggot!*

Drinking more, I watched replies pour in, first all negative, but then some supportive (although mostly from people with MAGA avatars).

When I woke up the next afternoon, still hungover and having forgotten all this, I opened Twitter and felt so shocked that I dropped my phone, cracking the already-scratched screen.

Desperate to delete the tweet, I tried logging on but was informed that I'd been locked out of my account for violating the terms of service.

And then I got the email.

Subject line blank, it said, "You love to tweet about how empty you are, how sad, how nothing is your fault and everyone should feel sorry for you."

"Yeah, so?" I responded aloud.

"Now," the email said, "you'll know what it feels like to actually be empty. To be erased."

I tried ignoring it.

Besides, I was late for my dentist appointment.

Then I noticed my missing ear lobes while looking in

the bathroom mirror, and screamed.

That was a week ago. Now my legs are also gone—only wagging nubs in their place, like vestigial tails.

I wonder what will be gone tomorrow. All of me, hopefully. I'm sick of feeling fat, and feeling in general.

I tweet from my new account: *it's really unfair that you put an ironic vanishing spell on me, yet the vanishing couldn't start with this tire around my waist.*

Someone replies: *you would sooner lose your mind than lose one pound.*

While that tweet racks up likes, another person adds: *your stomach—that's the one place you'll never be empty.*

"These unrealistic beauty standards are killing me," I say, between bites of bacon cheeseburger.

I don't remember getting the burger.

I say, or tweet (I can no longer tell the difference): *I think parts of my brain have started to vanish.*

Someone replies: *that would imply you had a brain to begin with.*

I try responding, but now my mouth is gone too.

If it weren't, though, I know I'd be smiling.

Because soon I'll be able to log off for good.

Conference-Called to Heaven

So I finally find a corporate job, but one day in the middle of a meeting about email etiquette, I start screaming.

The meeting was scheduled because our now-former CEO accidentally sent a dick pic to the whole team. It was a nice dick, I'm not gonna lie. When I compare it to mine, I can see why Grant gets—got—to be CEO.

But now I find myself screaming, and the whole room's looking at me like I've ripped off my shirt to reveal a suicide bomber vest. Or even just my own flabby body. Equally horrifying.

"Mason," says the HR rep, reading it from my name tag, "is everything all right?"

Everyone waits expectantly for me to say I'm fine and then sit back down. There are only a few PowerPoint slides left, and it's almost lunch time.

Instead of sitting down, I pick up the projector, ripping out its cords, planning to throw it at the wall. But it's so heavy—and I'm so weak—that it slips from my hands and onto the table. Everyone stands and backs away.

"Security!" the HR rep yells.

"They won't just appear," says Angela from Accounting. "You have to actually, like, call them."

The HR rep glowers.

Angela shrugs and dials the conference phone, somehow so calm while everyone else is freaking out, staring at me like I've gone crazy, which I guess I have. "We have an incident in conference room nine," she says.

"This is conference room eight." My boss, Carolyn, then turns to me and says, "Mason, put down the remote."

I am now pointing the little projector remote at my temple, like a gun. "Bang, bang, bang," I say.

An alarm goes off.

"Is that because of this?" someone asks. "Or is there an actual fire?"

A voice on the conference phone responds: "There's an actual fire."

"It's really unfair," I say, "that my breakdown gets overshadowed by some fire."

Then everyone's phones chime. It's an Instagram story from Grant. "I'm burning this place down," he says, looking hot.

"Should we evacuate?" the HR rep asks.

But we don't make it in time.

The ceiling collapses.

All of us are dead.

The smoke clears. We find ourselves in a vast hallway, waiting outside conference room 777. Jesus is presenting a PowerPoint about Scripture to the Apostles.

"Should we go in?" I ask.

"How is it that you got to Heaven with us, you crazy asshole?!" Angela exclaims.

"This is terrible," Carolyn says. "I didn't even get to eat lunch."

While my coworkers grumble, I enter conference room 777.

All the Apostles (besides Judas) turn to look at me.

"My son," Jesus says, "this conference room is booked."

"Not anymore," I say. I'm still holding the projector remote. I point it at Jesus and say, "bang, bang, bang."

Jesus collapses.

"Fuck," Judas says. "You beat me to it."

Three days later, I'm still getting used to Heaven. It's not much better than actual life. Same shitty job, minus a few coworkers who survived Grant's fire. The food sucks, and the angels won't stop singing.

I'm in my postmortem apartment, trying to find porn that hasn't been blocked by Heaven's internet filter, when there's a knock at the door.

Jesus is outside, looking pissed AF.

"You killed me!" Jesus screams.

I shrug. "Isn't forgiveness your whole thing?"

Jesus sighs. "I can't tell the difference between being forgiving and being a doormat."

"Well," I say, "I guess if I do something bad once, you should forgive me, but if I do it again, you shouldn't."

Jesus nods. "All right."

As he's walking away, I shoot Jesus again. Bang, bang, bang.

Someone really should have taken this remote from me.

So I end up in hell.

It's another office building, but with slippery tile and a thermostat set to broil. I pass Grant in the hallway. He is clutching a wound where his dick used to be. I say hi, and he whimpers in response.

In Conference Room 666, I settle in for a PowerPoint that, this time, is literally never-ending.

I try to scream, but all that comes out is a yawn.

Signs Point to Yes

Stoned in my car on the way to work, I whisper, "I feel scared... all the time."

Siri says, "I found ten thousand results for 'I feel scared all the time.'"

Behind the register, I start crying. Maybe because I just got evicted, maybe because I'm selling clothes and I hate clothes.

A customer, clutching a crinkled store bag, comes up to me and asks, "Are you okay?"

"No," I say.

The customer hands me the bag. "I need to return this."

I process the return, hand the customer tear-stained bills.

He wipes the wet money on his jeans and says, "Yuck."

I'm driving around in the rain, all my belongings in my trunk. I pass a billboard for liposuction and a billboard for fast food.

The sky is gloomy, like my mood.

"'It was a dark and stormy night,'" I say, not sure what I'm quoting.

Siri says, "I found one million results for..."

I'm at my friend Caitlin's place.

"Thanks for letting me crash," I say.

Wherever I go, I'm crashing.

Caitlin says, "No problem, we've got plenty of room."

And she does. I feel like she's mocking me with her spacious, cute apartment. I'm glaring at an accent wall when Caitlin's girlfriend asks, "How long do you think you might stay?"

At work the next morning, I bring my manager coffee and a donut.

"Thanks," he says, eyeing me suspiciously.

"So, I was just wondering, could I pick up an extra shift or two? I could really use the money."

"That depends," my manager says. "Are you going to keep bursting into tears?"

I pass the homeless guy who loiters outside. Today's sign reads: *Please Help—I'm a Veteran.*

"I'm homeless now, too," I tell him.

"Very funny," he says. "Do you have any more donuts?"

"No," I say, "but I think I have a dollar."

I dig around in my pockets.

All I can find is a dime.

"Thanks a lot," he says.

I call my father and tell him I got evicted again.

"You did this to yourself," he says. "All that money wasted on drugs."

I say, "That's absurd," and hang up.

I take a short detour on the way back to Caitlin's.

I drive past my apartment's front office, just to flip it off. I pretend my landlord can see me.

It doesn't really help.

I'm eating vegan pizza with Caitlin and her girlfriend. It tastes as bad as I feel.

The girlfriend notices my slow, disgusted chewing.

"Yeahhhh," she says, with heavy vocal fry, "normally I like this pizza, but I've had the strangest taste in my mouth all day."

"I think it tastes alright," Caitlin says.

The girlfriend says, "But, babe, you'll eat anything," and they laugh cutely, and I imagine murdering them both.

Once they're in bed, I go out onto their balcony. I look up at planes flying where stars should be.

I suck on my empty vape pen, wishing that I had a different life. Or at least more weed.

"I feel like dying," I say.

Siri says, "Did you mean 'I Feel Like Dying' by Lil Wayne?"

It sounds like a bad life, right? Depressed, evicted, underemployed. Maybe you feel sorry for me. But would your opinion change if you knew what I left out?

That every time I pass the homeless guy, I think, *At least you don't have to work retail.*

That I did use the rent money my dad gave me to buy weed.

And that last night I dipped Caitlin's girlfriend's toothbrush in the toilet.

"Siri," I ask, "am I a bad person?"

Before she can answer, I turn off my phone.

Are These Symptoms
or Am I Just an Asshole?

same shit, different therapist

# # #

#BPD #MDD #GAD #FML #KMS

# # #

how about less dopaYOURS and more dopaMINE?

# # #

looking for new ways to torture myself, because I'm too
numb for the old ones to hurt

# # #

if you're terrified of being abandoned, but it seems to
happen all the time… you might be a borderline!

# # #

I'm ready to be past tense

# # #

my body is an animal prison for a broken computer

# # #

you say potato, I say depression

# # #

what's the difference between
my personality and my disorder?

# # #

the picture of how I'm fucked up gets larger and clearer
and harder to erase, and I'm running out of canvas to
paint something else

# # #

give me dopamine or give me dissociation

# # #

if all your relationships are "love / hate" relationships…
you might be a borderline!

# # #

we accept the diagnoses we think we deserve

# # #

anyone got a hook-up for the Kevorkian drugs?

# # #

I don't just have major depression,
I majored in depression

# # #

bumper sticker on my ass:
"my other body isn't full of crazy"

# # #

getting to that "offer all my savings
for someone to kill me" point again

# # #

stare into the abyss and the abyss doesn't do anything,
because the abyss doesn't care

# # #

if you try on identities like hats, but can't ever find one
that fits... you might be a borderline!

# # #

"Wish You Never Had Me!" and Other Texts to Mom

# # #

screaming at pharmacist
we're going to need a bigger refill!

# # #

I need some time-away-from-me time

# # #

In Cognitive Distortions We Trust

# # #

I always feel anxious about X and depressed about Y...
the variables change, but the feelings never do

# # #

YOU:
dual-diagnosis

ME:
dueling diagnoses

# # #

wherever I go, there I am depressed

# # #

if you're reckless and impulsive, prone to breaking rules
and abusing substances... you may have been arrested!
(and you might be a borderline)

# # #

empty is the wrong word, since it implies
a capacity to be filled

# # #

drove behind a truck hauling a ladder on the tollway,
hoping the ladder would fly out and impale me
à la *Final Destination*

###

the self-doubt became self-loathing
and the self-loathing became dull

###

I was born alive, but I identify as dead

###

can I still call it a crisis if it's been going on for years?

###

endorphins are a myth created by
the exercise industrial complex

###

if you don't just have mood swings, you have entire mood
playgrounds… you might be a borderline!

###

I've got an amygdala that just won't quit

###

when people tell me to "hang in there,"
I always picture a noose

###

BPD is like feeling every feeling at once—opposite feelings simultaneously—and you feel them all the time

\# \# \#

if stress makes you paranoid,
like everyone's out to get you...
don't look behind you, but
you might be a borderline!

\# \# \#

schools should teach coping skills instead of geometry

\# \# \#

I'll show you my PHQ-9 if you show me yours first

\# \# \#

according to multiple studies in top scientific journals,
everyone else is happier, sexier and more successful
than I am

\# \# \#

looking for coping skills in a box of defense mechanisms

\# \# \#

am I allowed to be hateful if I meditate first?

\# \# \#

losing interest in my loss of interest

\# \# \#

it's not you, it's madness

#

I can't tell the difference between having
an epiphany and having a delusion

#

I'm always thinking I need to change everything all at
once instantly instead of one thing at a time

#

I don't want to have a "personality disorder." It's hard
enough getting people to take depression or anxiety seri-
ously, but a fucking "personality disorder"? it sounds
made up, like something that will be out of the psychia-
trists' manual in no time... same way doctors used to believe in hysteria, or that homosexuality was a disease

#

the light at the end of the tunnel is red, and I'm running it

#

YOU:
has issues

ME:
has volumes

#

I miss the food at the mental hospital

#

borderline? more like crossed-the-line

# # #

don't get me started on my "chronic feelings of
emptiness" unless you also want to hear about
my "recurrent suicidal thoughts"

# # #

out of the closet and into my feelings

# # #

I found my authentic self(-hatred)

# # #

on the transplant list for a new brain

# # #

whenever I check in with myself,
I'm immediately ready to check out

# # #

therapy? $150/appt
hospitalization? $20k
never getting better? priceless

# # #

executive producer of my own demise

# # #

have anxiety, won't travel

# # #

how many borderlines does it take to change a lightbulb?
no matter how many you get,
they will never feel like enough

# # #

every day is "bring your mental illness to work" day

# # #

I'm an incon (involuntarily conscious)

# # #

got my MFA in ambivalence

# # #

I'm whatever is beneath a downward spiral

# # #

one night of sleep is evidently too many, and a thousand
years of sleep would never be enough

# # #

save a borderline—kill a narcissist!

# # #

when people say, "hope you feel better," what they really
mean is: "I don't want to hear about it if you don't"

#

in Soviet Russia, you attack panic

#

who wants to fill up my pill organizer?
extremely Tom Sawyer voice it's *loads* of fun

#

keep looking for my plug so I can pull it

#

people say that being around a borderline is like "walking on eggshells," but they don't understand that *being* a borderline is like walking on quicksand that can turn into lava

#

dying alone is fine—it's living alone that sucks

#

how can I outsource self-care?

#

I keep thinking of different things to do
and wondering, *would that make me happy?*
and the answer is always "no"

#

I would say I'm losing it, but I never had it

#

am I eligible for hospice yet?

#

despite pop-culture portrayal, being a borderline only *occasionally* involves wielding knives at our ex-lovers…
(that being said, I do feel like my attractions are fatal)

#

found a weighted blanket on sale,
hope it solves all my problems

#

when all you have is a diagnosis,
everything looks like a symptom ↖

#

I'm bringing ~~sexy~~ melancholia back

#

might start referring to my borderline
personality disorder as my husband

#

this too shall pass (painfully, like a kidney stone)

#

borne back ceaselessly into the bullshit

#

would fewer people be depressed and anxious if they were in touch with their feelings, or does being too in touch with your feelings lead to depression and anxiety?

#

I'm emotionally gassy

#

how many times do I have to
destroy myself before it sticks?

#

knock, knock

"who's there?"

borderline.

"borderline who?"

I don't know, I have no sense of self

#

if I were Sisyphus, I'd just let the boulder crush me

#

ready for death to be the period on my life sentence

#

more like UN-Wellbutrin, am I right?

# # #

all the people lecturing you to feel better have been
getting laid and just want you to shut up

# # #

I can't tell the difference between
emotional support and emotional labor

# # #

"you got your depression in my anxiety!"
"no, you got your anxiety in my depression!"

# # #

(it's the abandonment, stupid)

# # #

sometimes I feel frustrated about people not wanting to
be around me because of my BPD... but then I interact
with another borderline, and it's like, *oh yeah, we are
fucking exhausting*

# # #

something has to change...
and that something is unfortunately me

# # #

no, there is nothing that "helps"

# # #

excited to announce
the forthcoming publication
of my obituary

# # #

paranoia is like gambling:
even if you only win (even if you're only right) 1 out of a
100 times, you know you'll risk more

# # #

my memory is terrible and so are my memories

# # #

found my inner child and left him at a fire station

# # #

the meds may not work but when I try to quit them
I feel even worse

# # #

when people say, "reach out to me anytime,"
what they really mean is:
"don't do this more than once or twice a year"

# # #

mounting a cross and nailing myself to it

# # #

When Anxiety Attacks

# # #

sings ["Closing Time"]
borderline
time for me to lash out
at the people I get love from
borderline
my mind won't be open,
cuz I'm screaming or I'm feeling numb
I gather up my regrets
and bring them to my doctors
I wish that I'd found a friend
borderline
you say new beginning,
I say let's just skip straight to the end

# # #

give us each day our daily meds

# # #

feel like an unpaid intern for my mental illness

# # #

practicing transcendental rumination

# # #

Portrait of the Not-Really-an-Artist
as a Not-So-Young-Anymore Piece of Shit

# # #

is there such a thing as NON-suicidal ideation?

# # #

abused & admonished & ambushed & anguished &
appalled & arrested & assassinated & autopsied
by anxiety

# # #

blame it on the bi- bi- bi- bi- bi-
biopsychosocial model of development

# # #

YOU: Major Depression

ME: Colonel Depression

# # #

the great person I want to be is like a hostage
trapped inside the shitty person I am now

# # #

why did the borderline cross the road?
because you crossed the road first,
and the borderline felt abandoned

# # #

maybe I'm already dead, but you
can't see it yet—like a star

# # #

YOU: *has episodes*

ME: *has marathons*

# # #

my thoughts are so loud,
I forget everyone can't hear them

# # #

know thyself? no thanks

# # #

insanity is repeating that quote about insanity's definition
as if this time it will be clever

# # #

am I a victim of brain chemistry who deserves love,
or a maniacal manipulator who deserves nothing?

# # #

ME:
don't define me by my diagnoses

ALSO ME:
don't forget about my diagnoses

Probably I'm the Only Person in the World to Fake Drunk Dialing

"You called him thirty times? Were you drunk or something?" my friend asks the next morning. It can feel like being drunk sometimes, the mood I get in. The total loss of control. The disembodied, screaming voicemails. Eyes obnoxious with tears. The nausea of needing to exorcise, being unable. "Yeah, I was completely fucked up," I say, not really lying.

Pop Quiz Taped to the Door of Your Apartment

TRUE/FALSE

1. We had plans to Netflix and chill.

        TRUE   FALSE

2. You never showed up.

        TRUE   FALSE

SHORT ANSWER (1-2 sentences each)

3. What, to you, constitutes setting a plan with someone? Are there any rules? Do you always reserve the right to cancel without calling/texting?

4. When you don't answer my phone calls, especially when we have plans, why do you get mad at me for texting? (Consider: I wouldn't text if you answered the phone.)

5. At what point did you decide that you weren't coming over? Did you think that you should call or text to notify me of your cancellation at that time? Why or why not? Be specific.

6. By doing these things, are you trying to "get back at me" for something in a passive-aggressive way? If so, what are you trying to get back at me for? Is it the mere fact that I have expectations of you?

7. Why is it so hard for you to simply call or text? Why does such a small courtesy feel like a huge burden?

8. Discuss your understanding (if any) of:
a)   how badly I miss you
b)   what your words mean to me
c)   what commitment means to you

9. Do you resent me for how much I care about you? Do you recognize how you use that care against me?

ESSAY QUESTION
10. Does love mean anything to you at all?

BONUS (∞ points)
When can I see you again?

My Favorite Person's Least Favorite Person Is Me

PROLOGUE

I'm Always Trying to Fill My God-shaped (ass)Hole

ME: I feel so lucky to have met you.

FP: ...

ME: Grindr usually sucks, but this time I hit the jack-pot.

FP: ...

ME: We have so much in common: writing... films...

FP: ...

ME: Plus, you're so fucking hot.

FP: Are we going to have sex now, or what?

ACT ONE

I've Been Ready for Marriage since Kindergarten,
But I'm still Not Ready to Date

ME: *2 Requiem 2 Dream.*

FP: *Mulholland Drive: Tokyo Drift.*

ME: *Antichrist 2: Satanic Boogaloo.*

FP: *An American Psycho in Paris.*

ME: Could we take a break from sequel puns and talk about where this relationship is going?

FP: I already told you—I don't do relationships.

ME: Right...

FP: ...

ME: *Trainspotting 2: Back on the Habit.*

ME: Sometimes I feel like such a poseur compared to real writers like you.

FP: What do you mean? I liked that script you showed me. I mean, for a sitcom.

ME: Yeah, thanks... but that was from a few years ago.

FP: So what have you written lately?

ME: Mostly tweets, I guess?
FP: ...

ME: I sit on the toilet a lot... with the exhaust fan on. It's the closest thing I have to a meditation room.
FP: That's kind of disgusting.
ME: [*sighs*] I know.

ME: I hate politics.
FP: But everything is political. It's all politics.
ME: Then I guess I hate everything. Except, of course, for you...
FP: ...

ME: I worry every time I fill up my car that I've parked too far from the pump, that the hose won't reach my tank. But it almost always does.
FP: ...
ME: Seems metaphorical, right?

ME: I wrote a poem for you.
FP: Cool.
ME: Backsliding, backtracking
I can't stop relapsing
You're brain dynamite and
My skull keeps collapsing

I'm hung up, left hanging
Forgive my haranguing

> I know we're not boyfriends
> But damn I love banging!

FP: Hmm...

ME: What'd you think?

FP: Aren't rhymes kind of cliché?

ME: But I love rhyming. It makes the words seem like they belong together. Like us.

FP: ...

ACT TWO

I Don't Have Crushes, I Have Obliterations

ME: *The eBook of Mormon.*

FP: *The Phantom of the Opera Browser.*

ME: *The Content Producers.*

FP: *Hamiltonline.*

ME: Have I told you how much I enjoy our pun-athons?

FP: You tell me constantly.

ME: You like them too, right?

FP: ...

ME: Hey, um, not to be annoying or anything, but I noticed that you were tweeting earlier... when you weren't texting me back.

FP: Yeah, so what?

ME: Well, if you had your phone... and you had time to tweet... then why didn't you have time to text me back?

FP: It's not a lack of time that's the problem.

ME: I feel like my body is half BPD, half fat.
FP: ...
ME: You're not going to disagree? To try and make me feel better?
FP: Maybe it's 60/40?

ME: Could I pick the movie this time? Maybe something less weird?
FP: Why would I want to watch anything I'm not interested in?
ME: But I watch the movies you want to watch all the time.
FP: Well, no one's forcing you.
ME: *Koyaanisqatsi* it is.

ME: Emotions are the "bad touch" of the mind.
FP: ...
ME: That's why they're called feelings.
FP: Stop it.

ME: I know I've been kinda annoying lately, so I wrote you another poem.
FP: Okay...
ME: I panic you hate me
                I push you away
                I text you to death and
                I'm never okay

I beg for forgiveness
then fuck up again
I'm not even comfortable
in my own skin

I want you to love me
I say I love you
So I will try harder
To prove my love true

FP: I don't know what's worse—your neediness, or
these poems.

ACT THREE

Too Bad I Didn't Spring for the Relationship Insurance

ME: *Bareback Mountin'.*

FP: …

ME: *There Will Be Cum.*

FP: …

ME: *Django Uncircumcised.*

FP: I don't want to see you anymore.

ME: Didn't our time together mean anything?

FP: I told you from the start—I didn't want this.

ME: Then why did you go along with it?

FP: What was I supposed to do?

ME: Okay, look, I know I'm hard to be with. But you can't possibly hate me more than I already hate myself.

FP: Wanna bet?

ME: Please, give me another chance.

FP: All I've done is give you chances.

ME: So why can't I have one more?

FP: I found someone better. Someone not crazy.

ME: I wish instead of meeting you I'd gotten cancer or
       something, because cancer would have fucked me
       up less.

FP: Do you realize how insensitive that is to people
       who've actually had cancer?

ME: I just wish people were as sympathetic to emo-
       tional problems as they are to physical ones.

FP: You expect everyone to feel sorry for you—when
       you're the one who fucked up.

ME: I'm not a person, but the shell of one
                   seeking a guy like you to make me whole
                   The more I want, the more you want to run

                   I'm told I shouldn't treat love like a goal
                   If I were a human, I'd be good.
                   I'd text and not care if you texted back
                   I'd feel secure in my own personhood
                   I wouldn't answer absence with attack

                   But as a shell, my routine rarely varies
                   once I'm attached, then you become a drug
                   what potency your every action carries
                   each text a hit, a high from each new hug

> I'm not a person, I'm a black hole only
> as a void, all I can feel is lonely

FP: If I hadn't already dumped you, I would have dumped you over that.

ME: You didn't like that one either? It's a sonnet, the rhymes are *supposed* to be there.

FP: But who the fuck would want to date a black hole?

EPILOGUE

We Were Canceled Years Ago,
But I Still Watch the Reruns

ME: Even though we were bad for each other, I miss you all the time.

FP: I don't think of you at all.

ME: Never? Then why do you keep talking to me?

FP: Because you keep bothering me. What's it going to take for you to move on?

ME: ...

(fade to black)

Last Call

At the bar you're not invited to, we all meet and laugh.

Instead of sports, we watch your life.

We watch you re-watching *The Office* on your flat-screen TV, chuckling and scratching your ass.

We watch you scrolling Instagram and Twitter, stuffing your face with snacks.

We watch you jerking off, and we snicker and point and say "ewww."

We watch as your sorrow grows as big as your gut, and we cheer and toast to your tears.

There are only a few of us at first.

Disappointed teachers.

Sneering coaches.

Fed-up friends.

But the crowd grows daily.

There's the preacher you questioned, the classmates you pestered, the commuters you cut off.

And of course your traumatized ex. Embarrassed and apologizing, baffled that they ever—even for a moment—thought that you were hot.

Always new faces, all of us watching, swapping stories and sharing drinks, making friends while we wait, wondering how long this will last.

Other than your parents, you've got only one supporter left: a remarkably kind friend from high school.

But even they eventually have enough.

One night, after hours of listening to you rant about your last ex, your "inexplicable" weight gain, your stalled career—after hours of you shooting down their every helpful hint, every suggestion to get better or to talk about something else—this final friend joins us in the bar.

With the help of some coworkers who've also been avoiding you, a schedule gets drawn up. A kind of "chore wheel" is constructed. The loser has to spend time with you, be your designated coworker or friend, to feign support as you weep and whine, rehash and regret.

Whenever you're not looking, they flip you off and roll their eyes.

We try to entertain ourselves.

Like fans at a midnight movie, we call out responses to your daily complaints, your favorite lines.

"Why am I depressed?" you ask.

We raise our glasses: "Your attitude stinks!"

"Why does everyone leave?" you ask.

We down our shots: "You drive us to drink!"

Someone eventually starts cutting together clip shows of your pratfalls; your farts; your pathetic attempts at sex. Sped up and set to wacky songs, they're almost amusing—instead of just sad.

But we are getting restless.

At the bar you're not invited to, we wait for you to die.

Your suicide attempts are our Super Bowl Sundays. You keep trying to OD, taking a few more pills each time, though you always end up calling 911.

After your third hospitalization, your parents finally join our viewing party. They held out as long as they could. They now watch you on screen as you tell the doctors that you're sorry.

Your dad says, "If you're sorry, why do you do it?"

Your mom sighs, and they both sip margaritas.

One night, we can tell that you're going to try again.

You choke down Xanax and strawberry Smirnoff, start scribbling your suicide note—the same boring shit— which is written so often now that we have a poster of it next to the dartboard of your face.

Your ex walks around, collecting our wagers.

After all the false alarms, only two people bet that this will be the attempt that actually kills you.

However, you've added a twist.

You tie a belt from your neck to the ceiling fan, and as you stand on your coffee table, we're on the edge of our seats.

Then the pills start kicking in. "Oh my god," you say, woozy and trembling, "what am I doing?"

You reach for the phone and trip, bringing a fan blade down with you.

We gasp as you collapse.

"Maybe this is it!" your ex shouts, embracing your replacement.

No luck.

You are screaming and thrashing about, hurt but alive.

The bar is filled with groans and what-the-fucks, like a quarterback fumbled the ball.

Your parents spin the chore wheel to see who has to meet you at the hospital.

Someone yells, "Turn it off!" and it becomes a chant—"Turn it off! Turn it off! Turn it off!"—so one of us reaches for the remote.

Then your psychiatrist says, "Wait! His TV! It's moving!"

Your flat-screen TV wobbles on the wall.

Reaching for something to pull yourself up, you grab the TV's power cord and yank.

The flat-screen falls, shattering into sparks and shards of glass.

Before we can react, our screens all cut to black.

"Is that it?" your old coach asks.

"I guess so," your third-grade teacher says.

"Hashtag cancelled!" your ex adds.

There's laughter all around, and scattered applause.

Your parents start crying, but we quickly realize their tears are happy ones; they were the two who bet you'd follow through, and they've won big.

"We can finally go on vacation!" your mom says.

She and your dad kiss, dreaming of Bermuda.

A few of us tear up, and "Closing Time" plays. We head out to live our lives, the way you never would.

Yet once we're gone, and the bar is empty, one screen flickers back to life.

I Thought I Was Crazy in Love, But I Was Just Crazy

should I make an OKCupid profile for the third time,
get incredibly discouraged then kill myself,
or should I skip OKCupid?

# # #

nobody: *loves me*

# # #

find someone who looks at you like I look
at guys who won't look at me

# # #

I know we just met, but I love you already,
so can you catch up?

# # #

I can't tell the difference between giving gifts
and buying someone off

# # #

hung up on him, and hung up on by him

# # #

keep dating ghosts and then acting surprised
when I get ghosted

# # #

*MTV True Life: I Fold My Blanket into a Person-Shaped
Lump So I Can Pretend I'm Holding Someone in Bed*

# # #

always the crushed, never the crusher

# # #

still awful at being alone despite decades of practice

# # #

chanting over cauldron hippity-hoppity-hex
I wish that we never had sex

# # #

shout out to all the couples tonight—as in, please
shout at them until they break up

# # #

*To All The Boys I've ~~Loved~~ Thought-I-Wanted-To-Be-
With-But-Really-Just-Wanted-To-Be Before*

# # #

one day I'll stop getting entangled with creepy guys
(probably when one of them kills me)

# # #

is it called Tinder because it
makes me want to start fires?

# # #

withering away like a plant everyone tells to water itself

# # #

when you get my hopes up for nothing,
that's a hate crime

I am like an insect—always flying toward the (gas)light

# # #

must love dogs, pretension, and long walks on my face

# # #

sings ["Mr. Downside"]
it started out with a text
how did I end up so vexed?
it was only a text
(it was ten million texts)

# # #

I'm my crazy exes' crazy ex

# # #

seeking a boyfriend like a garbage can seeks trash

# # #

trying to radically accept your rejection

# # #

feeling abandoned by people
who were never actually here

# # #

YOU:
wears your heart on your sleeve

ME:
*strips naked, cuts heart out of body and presents it
on a platter while screaming*

# # #

if you won't like me back, then at least like my tweets

# # #

all over him like obsession on compulsion

# # #

YOU:
"what are your pronouns?"

ME:
"I don't care what you call me, just call me!"

###

new Grindr profile:
"I want to be rode hard and put away dead"

###

when you screamed at me "I hate you,"
I heard it as "better luck next time"

###

to once be desired instead of just tolerated
would be fucking incredible

###

trying not to seem like I'm waiting for someone to love me
(while I wait for someone to love me)

###

I think I feel about Valentine's Day the way infertile wom-
en feel about Mother's Day

###

RELATIONSHIP TWITTER:
"fuck anyone who's ever made you feel
like you're hard to love"

ME:
"I *exclusively* fuck people who make me feel
like I'm hard to love"

###

it's called OKCupid because it's not bad,
but it's definitely not great

# # #

all roads lead to abandonment,
and I'm in a race car

# # #

ending a phone call by interrupting me to say, "hey, I'm
gonna let you go"—"let me go," like he's doing me a favor

# # #

once a guy was nice to me, and I've been
in withdrawal ever since

# # #

new Tinder profile:
"looking for a victim, I mean boyfriend"

# # #

so unfair that exes keep existing after their exits

# # #

didn't realize just how far gone my own appearance
was 'til I saw the guy my friend thought I'd be
a "good match" for

# # #

when I told you I could handle being
friends with benefits, I lied

###

no one will fall for me no matter how much I trip them

###

when I say I can't wait to see you, I mean it just as much
as when I say I hope I never see you again

###

Threnody to the Victims of My Affection

###

but what if I just texted to make sure
he was getting all my texts?

###

brb turning people into drugs

###

so ready for someone to invent the relationship-
memory-erasing machine from *Eternal Sunshine
of the Spotless Mind*

###

find someone who looks at you like I look
at people who won't look at me

###

some people fall out of love, but you jumped

#

a tub of codependency labeled
I Can't Believe It's Not Love!

#

I have apology tours the way Cher has farewell tours

#

closure is a myth, but text me back

#

sure wish I had known beforehand that
our last time was the last "last time"

#

I never remember to cross bridges before burning them

#

holy commitment issues, Batman!

#

when I do it, it's "manipulation,"
but when you do it, it's "self-care"

#

loves self for fifteen seconds ok, I'm a whole person…
now will you go out with me?

# # #

kind of just waiting to see which expires first:
my unopened box of condoms, or me

# # #

I've caught the feels
like slinking eels
that wrap around my neck
I'm out of air
I'll see you there
I'm already a wreck

# # #

I'll be Romeo and you be the poison

# # #

how do people make friends?
(asking for a friend)

# # #

this relationship is going to work,
even if it kills us both

# # #

kissing a lot of frogs to find my prince
does not work when I too am a frog

# # #

too bad that condoms don't protect against emotions

# # #

what's wrong with wanting unconditional love
from guys I barely know?

# # #

can't wait until I have enough self-esteem
to stop seeing you

# # #

future-me has a devoted partner,
but present-me only swipes left

# # #

yes I'm desperately alone,
no I can't stand anyone

# # #

why haven't you answered my
"don't talk to me ever again" text?

# # #

kind of want to go clubbing,
kind of want to club myself

# # #

every time I think I'm over it,
I realize I'm still under it

# # #

how about this time your heart gets broken instead?

#

stare into the abyss and the abyss is like
"have you met my new boyfriend?"

#

American Horror Story: Left on Read

#

fingers crossed my wit makes up for my unlovability

#

ME:
hey Siri, if neither of us are married
by the time we're 40...

SIRI:
no

#

a panic a day keeps a boyfriend away

#

you had me at "hell no"

#

I thought breaking up and getting back together was
romantic, because it only happens in love stories to
couples who are "meant to be"

#

I don't want to hang out, but
I want you to want to hang out

#

I'm sorry in the streets, I'm sorry in the sheets

#

under what conditions would you
love me unconditionally?

#

suck my codependency

#

dreaming of old "you"s

#

I'll be really missing someone, but then when I go see
them, I end up leaving early and disappointed—only to
start missing them again on the drive home

#

will someone start a business with me
so I can tell people I have a partner?

#

attracted to people who find me repulsive /
repulsed by people who find me attractive

###

jealous of people who abandon me for having that option

###

is that an attachment disorder in your pocket,
or are you just ambivalent about seeing me?

###

if I saw you all the time then I wouldn't have to
bother you about when I'll see you next

###

All the Reasons You Should Take Me Back, Even Though
You Hate Me and Won't Read This: A THREAD

###

how old can you get before it stops being okay
you haven't had a "real" relationship yet?

###

I'm both fucked and unfuckable

###

YOU: promiscuous

ME: amateur-miscuous

###

when people say, "you have to love yourself," I hear, "you have to love yourself—because none of us are gonna love you, you dysfunctional asshole"

# # #

the more you know me, the less you'll like me

# # #

"nice axe! my name's Giving Tree..."—me on dating apps

# # #

can someone please just come over for a few minutes and then never leave?

# # #

MTV True Life: The Only Ways I Know How to Show Love Are the Same Things That Make Me Unlovable

# # #

always bawling, never balling

# # #

no one will commit to me and I should be committed

# # #

the guy who took my virginity also took my sanity

# # #

sorry for forcing you to gaslight me

###

come for the anxious negativity,
stay for the overwhelming clinginess!

###

I'll believe anything you say about me
as long as it's not good

###

does it still count as passive aggressive
if I did it out of love?

###

can't fight the suspicion that all my personality flaws
would be overlooked if my BMI were 19 instead of 29

###

tried to love myself, but myself swiped left

###

hanging on by a pube

###

don't share the things you love with the guy you're dating,
unless you're prepared to watch him enjoy those same
things with your replacement

###

I wish I could like you less so that you would like me more

# # #

instead of throwing myself at you,
I should have thrown myself into the ocean

# # #

no one has ever been that into me

# # #

the worst part of being gay is the men

# # #

skinning my knees on the pavement of your indifference

# # #

sings [theme to *The Mary Tyler Moore Show*]
love is all around
but why should I try?
anyone I like
I just get left by
I'll never find love after all
tosses my decapitated head into the air

# # #

don't you DARE respond to OR ignore me

# # #

I'd settle for a soul acquaintance

# # #

who doesn't feel you makes you stronger

# # #

keep mistaking people who use me
for people who want me

# # #

afraid no one will ever love me besides my parents,
who basically have to

# # #

I may not be charming, but at least I'm no fun

# # #

...and the thirstier you are, the less attractive that you
seem, but the less attractive that you seem, the thirstier
that you become...

# # #

ME:
wish I could write another script
instead of these pathetic tweets

FP:
me, too

THE SHOW

a pilot

by

Marshall Crawford

ACT ONE

INT. HOTEL ROOM
Movie posters, family photos... Someone
lives in this hotel.

BATHROOM
MAX COLLINS (20s, gay) sits on the TOILET
looking bland and overweight. He's too
fat/hairy to be a twink, but not fat/hairy
enough to be a bear.

Between spurts of propulsive DIARRHEA, Max
studies the fine print on a box which reads
"ANAL DOUCHE."

                    MAX
"Gentle cleansing" my ass.

He tosses the box into the trash. He picks
up a VAPE PEN from the counter and takes a
hit of marijuana concentrate.

A beat as Max gets stoned. Then he
ADDRESSES US, taking a shit on the fourth
wall:

                    MAX
          (to us)
Normally, I don't bother douching. The anus
isn't a holding cell for poop, you know.

Max flushes the toilet, scrunches his face
briefly to FART, then speaks again --

                    MAX
              (to us)
But it's Nico. I want everything perfect.

LIVING ROOM - LATER
Max, dressed in an outfit that would give
the "Queer Eye" guys a stroke, sits on a
couch in what passes for his living room,
clearly nervous. He checks his phone, then
sets it aside.

He turns on the TV, tries to distract
himself. It doesn't work. He keeps checking
his phone, his impatience becoming full-on
panic. Finally, he can't wait anymore...

Max scrolls through a tiny list of Contacts
and calls NICO.

                    MAX
              (on phone)
Hey!

                    NICO
              (off-screen)
Hi...

                    MAX
Sorry to bother you, but I was just
wondering, since it's almost 6:00, if you
were still planning on --

                    NICO
              (off-screen)
...I'm not picking up right now. You know
what to do.

It's one of those obnoxious trick
voicemails.

Annoyed, Max almost throws his phone. He
struggles to compose himself before the
voicemail's prompting BEEP.

                    MAX
Hey, it's me... Max. So, it's almost time
for our dinner reservation, and you're not
here...

Max holds his hand over the phone and turns
to face us.

                    MAX
          (to us)
You know what? It's probably just a
misunderstanding... Nico thought we were
meeting at the restaurant, I thought he was
picking me up. I've gotta stop freaking out
about things.

Returning to his conversation, Max forces a
casual tone:

                    MAX
          (on phone)
Yeah, so, never mind, the thing I wanted to
check was... nothing. So... I'll just see
you there!

Max ends the call, then switches to his
phone's map for directions. He's headed for
a sushi bar, its logo a chopped-in-half,
grinning CARTOON FISH.

EXT. SUSHI BAR - NIGHT
The CARTOON FISH in neon above a sushi
bar's entrance.

INSIDE
Casual, colorful. We should be wondering
how Max even got a "reservation" -- it's
not that kind of place.

Alone at a table in the corner, Max fidgets
with his napkin.

                    WAITRESS
Still don't want anything?

Max jerks, startled by the waitress's
sudden appearance.

                    MAX
No thanks. I'm waiting for my date.

The waitress shakes her head like, if you
say so.

EXT. SUSHI BAR / STREET - LATER
Still alone, Max exits the sushi bar with a
bag of TAKE-OUT.

                    MAX
          (to us)
He never showed. I've called nineteen
times, but he hasn't answered once.

A beat.

                    MAX
            (to us)
Obviously, something terrible has happened.

Then Max looks PAST US, sees something that
ENRAGES him:

Outside a coffee shop across the street,
NICO (20s, sexy) -- the guy Max has been
waiting on -- is on a date with SOME OTHER
GUY.

(This is ESTEBAN: 20s, modelesque, "Queer
Eye"-approved.)

Max drops the take-out bag, dumping sushi
everywhere. He darts toward Nico, RUNNING
THROUGH TRAFFIC.

An SUV stops just short of HITTING him and
honks. Max and the driver flip each other
off, then Max continues SPRINTING...

EXT. COFFEE SHOP
Max has built up so much MOMENTUM that the
only way he can stop is by bracing himself
on Nico's table. He plants his arms on it,
landing hard, which causes Esteban's coffee
to SPILL everywhere.

                    ESTEBAN
            (re: coffee stains)
So much for my new Armani jeans...

                    NICO
What the fuck, Max?!

Max tries to look assertive while catching his breath.

                    MAX
What do you mean "What the fuck"?! It's our anniversary!

Nico snorts in disgust while Esteban looks amused.

                    ESTEBAN
          (to Nico)
You were right, he does look better in pictures than in person.

Esteban heads inside to deal with the coffee stain.

                    MAX
          (re: Esteban)
You replaced me already? We were still dating six weeks ago!

                    NICO
We were talking six weeks ago, and that's only because when we're not talking, you harass me. You --

                    MAX
Tonight was --

                    NICO
-- blow up my texts... flood my inbox... use fucking prank call websites just to see if I'll pick up my phone...

                    MAX
I haven't done that in --

                    NICO
I'm with someone better now. Someone not
crazy.

Max winces, wounded.

                    MAX
Can't we talk about --

                    NICO
All we ever did was talk!

                    MAX
That's not all we did...

Max looks hard at Nico, tries to let his
words land, but Nico won't have it. He's
ruffling through his pockets, grabbing a
pack of cigarettes.

                    MAX
Tonight would have been six months... I had
reservations at our place, and an
anniversary gift --

Nico scoffs.

                    NICO
Always trying to buy me shit, force me to
love you, like I'm some kind of fucking
prostitute.

                    MAX
That's not what I... I just thought that
it'd be... I was hoping that maybe...

                    NICO
What do I have to say to make you
understand that I don't want you?!

His face turning red, Max chokes back
tears. He starts to walk away, then
reconsiders:

                    MAX
          (to us)
Sure, I could give up now, but all the
great couples have broken up and gotten
back together... Ross and Rachel, Corey and
Topanga...

Resolved, he dramatically turns to Nico and
proclaims:

                    MAX
I'll never stop loving you.

Nico just laughs.

                    NICO
I've already forgotten you.

Off Max, DEVASTATED, we

                END ACT ONE

ACT TWO

EXT. ALLEY - NIGHT
Max falls to his knees by a Dumpster and
WEEPS for an uncomfortably long time.

Then he notices a crusty HOMELESS WOMAN
(40s) a few yards away, who's been WATCHING
Max's meltdown. The homeless woman waves.
Max waves back...

LATER
Max now smoking the WEED PEN he brings
everywhere, rants at the bored homeless
woman.

                    MAX
...just thought that it was one of those
things like the movies... You know, where
-- even though they haven't been talking in
a while -- the couple reunites at the spot
where they used to meet?

               HOMELESS WOMAN
Uh-huh...

                    MAX
I can't believe I let myself get so excited
over nothing... again. You know, every time
I get my hopes up, something bad happens.
My life fucking sucks.

The homeless woman glares at Max -- well-
fed and getting high, oblivious to his
privilege.

                    HOMELESS WOMAN
Well. Maybe you just haven't met the right
person yet.

Max takes this as an "a-ha!" moment.

                         MAX
Of course! I've got to meet someone else,
someone who won't take me for granted...

He starts walking away.

                    HOMELESS WOMAN
                    (pissed)
I listened for two hours... Not even some
loose change?!

INT. HOTEL LOBBY - NIGHT
Loose change, bills, receipts -- we're
looking at a CASH REGISTER on the hotel's
front desk.

The hotel's owner/manager, CAROLYN (50s),
counts money. She's tough, assertive, and
wearing a SILVER CHRISTIAN CROSS.

                      CAROLYN
                    (to herself)
Short fifty bucks... again.

Frowning, she SLAMS the cash register shut.

INT. GAY CLUB - NIGHT
In a packed gay dance club, a shirtless

BARTENDER slams his own cash register shut.

Max squeezes past writhing bodies to the
bar. He shouts to order a drink over the
deafening thumpa-thumpa of the music:

                    MAX
Vodka Red Bull.

                    BARTENDER
Eight bucks.

Max hands over a ten and looks around. He
notices two SHIRTLESS GUYS grinding on each
other a few yards away and gawks at them,
equally hungry and scared.

                    MAX
          (to bartender)
Can I get another one?

LATER
Several drinks later, a bleary-eyed Max
bobs his head to the music, off-beat.

                    MAX
          (to us)
Okay, here goes nothing...

Max half-stumbles, half-dances toward the
sweaty crowd, looking for a guy to
approach.

Finally he locates a target: BEARDED GUY
(20s).

                    MAX
               (loud)
          Hey, what's up?

                    BEARDED GUY
          What?

                    MAX
               (even louder)
          How's it... How are you?

          Bearded Guy looks at Max disdainfully.

                    BEARDED GUY
          No.

          Max looks like he's been slapped.

          LATER
          Back at the bar, Max is now full-on
          plastered.

          He spots a CUTE GUY (20s) coming up to
          order.

                    CUTE GUY
               (to Bartender)
          Can I get --

                    MAX
               (to Bartender)
          Oh, uh, hey, I'll pay for whatever he's
          getting.

          The Cute Guy looks over and Max smiles
          back.

CUTE GUY
Wow, thanks! My girlfriend was right -- you
guys are the best!
        (to Bartender)
Can I get two shots of Fireball and...

Max looks DISGUSTED, like he could scream.
Or like --

OUTSIDE THE GAY CLUB - MOMENTS LATER
Max runs out of the club and VOMITS.

                MAX
        (to us)
Yeah, so...
        (wiping his mouth)
Online dating it is...

INT. HOTEL LOBBY
At the front desk, Carolyn lectures an
employee, ANGELA.

                CAROLYN
I just don't think I can believe you
anymore, Angela. I'm sorry.

                ANGELA
But Mrs. Collins, I would never --

Carolyn shakes her head; the discussion's
over.

                CAROLYN
You'll be paid through the end of the week.

Angela scowls.

EXT. HOTEL
An Uber drops off Max, who's still drunk
and vomit-stained.

A gay hustler, BRADY (20s), stands near the
hotel's entrance, looking like one of the
hot mall guys posing outside an Abercrombie
& Fitch.

Max grins nervously, obviously attracted,
but too scared and drunk to speak. He heads

INT. HOTEL
Just as Angela is exiting. When she spots
him, she FLIPS HIM OFF with both middle
fingers before heading outside.

Looking more confused than upset, Max
approaches Carolyn at the front desk.

                    MAX
What was that all about?

                  CAROLYN
I had to let Angela go. The register was
short again.

                    MAX
You... You caught her stealing?

                  CAROLYN
No, but... Who else could it be?

Carolyn gives Max a long look... but if he
has something to hide, he's not giving it
up yet.

                    CAROLYN
              (notices his smell)
P-U! Someone's been drinking!

                    MAX
I've had a really shitty night.

                    CAROLYN
              (re: "shitty")
Language...!

                    MAX
Sorry, sorry. It's just, uh... really hard
to meet a nice girl.

(Note that he said "nice girl" -- Max isn't
"out" at work.)

                    CAROLYN
Oh, honey. I know you'll find a wife
someday.
              (then)
You're still on for your shift tomorrow,
though, right?

Max sighs heavily.

                    MAX
Yes, Mom.

(And now we understand why Max lives in a
hotel -- Carolyn, the hotel's
owner/manager, is his MOM.)

Max starts for the elevators as his mom
calls after him:

                    CAROLYN
Drink some water!

INT. HOTEL ROOM
An untouched GLASS OF WATER on the desk
beside Max's computer. He's working on an
online dating profile, scrolling through
page after page of "getting to know you"
questions.

                    MAX
              (to himself)
What do I do for fun?

He takes a hit from his weed pen.

Then, furtively, like he's about to look at
porn, he pulls up his "ex" Nico's
Instagram. In picture after picture, Nico
and Esteban are doing happy couple shit.

Max starts to spiral. He clicks through the
social media pages of one ex after another,
getting more and more upset.

                    MAX
              (to himself)
It's not just Nico... Every guy I've ever
dated has moved on. And half of them are
fucking engaged! Why can't I get a
boyfriend? What's so wrong with me?
              (MORE)

                    MAX (CONT'D)
          (to us)
Don't answer that.

Max clicks around, finds a SHIRTLESS
picture of Nico and Esteban on some beach.
He zooms in on Nico's abs, pushing Esteban
out of frame.

And then, Max slides a hand into his
pants... and, while crying, starts to
masturbate.

INT. HOTEL LOBBY — THE NEXT DAY
Max is slumped on the front desk in a dingy
uniform, hungover and half-asleep.

A beaming, affectionate STRAIGHT COUPLE
(20s) walks by, groping each other on their
way to the elevator.

                    MAX
          (to us)
Heterosexuals. Always throwing their love
in our face.

The front door chimes. Brady, the male
prostitute we saw earlier, enters with an
ugly middle-aged "client." Now alert and
intrigued, Max pulls himself together.

                    MAX
Good evening, gentlemen!

                    UGLY CLIENT
                 (almost whispering)
We're, uh, gonna need a room.

The Ugly Client exchanges cash for a hotel
room keycard.

                       MAX
Enjoy your stay!

The Ugly Client shuffles off, embarrassed.
Brady starts to follow...

But Max suddenly has an idea.

                       MAX
Hey, wait! Uh...

Brady turns back.

                      BRADY
Yes?

                       MAX
I'm Max. I've uh, seen you around...

                      BRADY
I've seen you around, too.

Max blushes, charmed.

                      BRADY
I'm Brady.

They shake hands.

                    MAX
So, basically, I was just wondering...
Um...

                    BRADY
Yes?

                    MAX
Well, I know that you're... Um...

                    BRADY
An escort?

                    MAX
Right... And I was just wondering if you
ever did, like, non-hooking-up things?

                    BRADY
You're asking if I ever do anything besides
fuck?

Max turns red.

                    MAX
I mean, not like, in a bad way, but... kind
of?
        (a beat)
I want to make someone jealous...

Brady flashes a wicked grin.

                    BRADY
I think I could help you out with that. I
should warn you, though -- I'm expensive.

                    MAX
Even if we don't... you know...?

                    BRADY
          (well-rehearsed)
You're paying for my time... regardless of
how we spend it.

                    MAX
Oh, okay.

Max looks at the cash register... considers
how far he's willing to go...

                    MAX
So how much are we talking, exactly?

                END ACT TWO

<u>ACT THREE</u>

EXT. HOTEL - THE NEXT DAY
A beautiful afternoon. Max waits outside
the hotel, looking at Instagram on his
phone.

ON HIS PHONE: A notification that Nico and
Esteban have "checked in" at the nearby
CITY ZOO.

Brady walks up and greets Max with a hug.

                    BRADY
So, where to?

Off Max's mischievous look, we're clearly
headed to...

EXT. THE ZOO
In a crowd of happy couples and families,
Max and Brady hold hands and explore the
zoo. Max, preoccupied, searches for any
sign of Nico and Esteban.

An OBESE MAN eyes Brady, who nods and
gestures toward the nearby BATHROOMS.

                    BRADY
I'll be right back, okay?

                    MAX
Uh-huh...

As Max looks around, oblivious, Brady is
visible in the BACKGROUND, where he meets
the Obese Man by a bathroom. As they chat,
Brady adds his number to the Obese Man's
phone.

Max continues searching... and searching...
until --

There! Max spots Nico and Esteban a few
yards away.

                    MAX
Hey! Nico!

Max pushes through the crowd. Nico and
Esteban, when they notice Max coming, make
the faces you'd expect.

                  ESTEBAN
Great. It's "Look Who's Stalking Too."

                    NICO
         (to Max)
What are you doing here?

                    MAX
I just wanted you to meet my new boyfriend.
Brady.

Nico and Esteban give each other a look.

                    NICO
Oh? And where is he?

For a moment, Max is defeated again -- but
then, just in time, Brady returns. He puts
his arm around Max and kisses him on the
cheek.

                    BRADY
Hey, babe, who's this?

                    MAX
          (maximum smugness)
Brady, meet Nico. Nico, Brady.

Nico is IN SHOCK. He obviously never
expected Max to land a guy as hot as Brady.

                    NICO
Nice to meet you...

Esteban is pissed to not be introduced.

                    ESTEBAN
And I'm Nico's boyfriend, Esteban...

                    NICO
          (gazing at Brady)
Right... This is Esteban...

Max beams. Mission accomplished.

                    MAX
Well, we'd better be going... busy day
ahead. I just wanted to say a quick hello.

                    ESTEBAN
Of course you did.

                    BRADY
Nice to meet y'all!

Brady leads Max away, kissing him once
again for show. Once they're safely out of
Nico's earshot:

                    BRADY
How was that?

                    MAX
Perfect.

Brady grins. But then he looks at the time
on his phone.

                    BRADY
So, it's been three hours....

                    MAX
And that's all the time we have?

                    BRADY
It doesn't have to be...

While Max ponders, the Homeless Woman from
before wanders up. She looks at Max, then
at Brady, with the same WTF expression Nico
had.

               HOMELESS WOMAN
          (bitterly)
Guess it all worked out for you, huh?

                    MAX
Do I know you?!
        (to Brady)
How did she get in here?

Brady shrugs, not looking up from his
phone.

                    BRADY
Yeah, so... I've really gotta get going...

                    MAX
But I have so many more exes to make
jealous.

                    BRADY
And I'm happy to help you. But a guy's
gotta eat.

                    MAX
        (re: Brady's toned physique)
As if you ever eat...

INT. HOTEL LOBBY
A sandwich sits half-eaten on the front
desk by Carolyn. She's checking the cash
register again, looking flustered.

And then Angela -- the employee Carolyn had
fired -- walks up, brandishing her phone
like a weapon.

                    CAROLYN
What are you doing h --

                    ANGELA
You need to see this.

Angela pulls up a video on her phone and
presses play. We can't see what it shows
just yet, but Carolyn's HORRIFIED
EXPRESSION tells us that it's something
upsetting...

EXT. HOTEL
Max and Brady walk up mid-conversation,
again holding hands.

                    BRADY
I'm glad we could work something out.

                    MAX
I just have to figure out how to get her
away from the desk for a few minutes...

                    BRADY
          (full flirt mode)
I have complete faith in you.

Almost delirious from praise, Max ambles

INT. HOTEL LOBBY
But then Max spots Angela, next to his
FURIOUS mother.

                    CAROLYN
Come. Over. Here!

Uh-oh. Suddenly Max looks like a criminal on Death Row. He hesitantly approaches his mother...

                    CAROLYN
NOW!

...then scrambles toward her.

                    MAX
Y-yes, Mom? What's... What's wrong?

                    CAROLYN
Don't give me that BS.

Max gasps -- for Carolyn, "BS" is the worst profanity.

                    CAROLYN
          (to Angela)
Show him.

Smirking proudly, Angela plays the video for Max... and now we get to watch it, too --

VIDEO ON SCREEN:
An awkward view of the HOTEL LOBBY, partially obscured by furniture, trees, etc. (Angela was secretly recording from some hiding place.)

At the front desk, Max and Brady flirt; it's the scene from yesterday, same as we saw before --

But then, Max looks around to check for witnesses.

Satisfied the coast is clear (and apparently not spotting Angela), Max opens the CASH REGISTER DRAWER...

He removes a stack of TWENTY-DOLLAR BILLS... and HANDS THE MONEY TO BRADY.
BACK TO HOTEL LOBBY

Max has been <u>caught</u>.

                    CAROLYN
How could you do this to me? To our family's business?

                    MAX
I... Uh...

                    CAROLYN
And who the <u>heck</u> was that guy you gave the money to?

                    MAX
Would you believe me if I said he was a... a professional matchmaker? Helping me find a girl you could be proud of?

Angela scoffs.

                    ANGELA
          (to Carolyn)
That guy is a prostitute. A <u>gay</u> prostitute.

Carolyn clutches her cross like it's a pearl necklace.

                    CAROLYN
What?!
        (to Max)
Why would you be talking to a -- a
homosexual?

Max pauses. Should he lie again, like
always? He looks outside at Brady, who
smiles.

No. Fuck it. Time to tell the truth:

                    MAX
Because, Mom. I am a homosexual.

Carolyn shrieks.

                    CAROLYN
I'm calling your father! And Pastor Todd!

Carolyn STORMS OFF in a huff.

                    MAX
        (to us)
Notice how she's more upset about me being
gay than me being a thief?

Angela chases after Carolyn.

                    ANGELA
Wait, Mrs. Collins! I have my job back,
right?

Max, now alone at the front desk, takes in
everything that just happened. He looks
outside at Brady again, catches his eye.

Brady taps an invisible watch on his wrist
-- a reminder that they're on the clock.

Max takes a deep breath. He opens the cash
register drawer...

...and he <u>empties</u> it entirely into his
pockets. Not just a few bucks this time --
HUNDREDS of dollars.

As if Max can see our response (what the
hell is he doing?!), he shrugs, looking
free for the first time.

                    MAX
             (to us)
YOLO, right?

Our thieving homosexual, now out and proud,
exits the hotel to join his prostitute, to
embark on a new life of adventure, as we

                FADE OUT.

Acknowledgements

Parts of this book appeared, in slightly different form, at *PANK*, *Soft Cartel*, *Philosophical Idiot*, *Maudlin House* and *Misery Tourism*.

Thank you to my parents, Oscar Enrique, Manzel Chapman, Melissa Broder, Brian Alan Ellis, Joe Halstead, Noah Cicero, Jennifer Wortman, Brooks Sterritt, Cathy Ulrich, Charlene Elsby, and Alison Ligocki for your support, kindness, and inspiration.

Joshua Dalton is a borderline writer living in Texas. This is his first book.

Printed in Great Britain
by Amazon